THE TENEBROUS MIND

Volume I

A Collection of Horror Stories

WILL LOWREY

THE TENEBROUS MIND
Copyright © 2019 by William C. Lowrey
All rights reserved.

Editing by Christie Moreton
Cover by Olivia Pro Design
Formatting by The Book Khaleesi

ISBN 978-1-7329399-7-4 (paperback)
Published by Lomack Publishing

www.lomackpublishing.com

First Edition

CONTENTS

To dreams and dreamers and all who let their mind run free.

THE GREEN WOODPECKER

THE GREEN WOODPECKER

We're chasing a ghost! Let's turn back," heaved Jakob, doubled at the waist and panting heavily in the thick, musky air.

Werner sighed deeply as he wiped the sweat from his brow. "We've come all the way back here and now you want to turn around," he panted. "Just a little while longer, Jakob."

The two boys had been on the hunt for the better part of the afternoon. They now found themselves deep in the forest as the sun set high above the crest of the pine trees. A faint, sweet aroma wafted through the base of the forest; the sap from the trees exuded a mildly pleasant scent which gave the woods an inherently inviting aura.

"Mum will have my hide if I don't get home soon, you know," rasped young Jakob, his words laced with a mix of exhaustion and frustration.

"And she'll give it right back once ya tell her what we've seen," offered Werner, turning to smile at the slightly younger boy.

Despite having only known each other a short while, the two boys had forged a strong bond, their common appetite for adventure and all things outdoors drew them together. Werner was slightly older, taller, and gangly with reddish hair, obligatory freckles, and a devilish grin. Jakob was a smaller boy, but stout and rugged as attested to whenever the larger boys taunted him, as they tended to for his curly hair and backwoods demeanor. Werner had moved here from a town in the next county just over a year ago with his parents and younger siblings. He took a quick liking to Jakob and the two would set out to play in the neighboring woods for hours on end, whiling the day away in the magic of the forest.

"We're gonna find it, Jakob. It's gonna be me and you, the ones who see it and don't you forget that," implored the older boy, encouraging his young friend.

Jakob could only shake his head. Standing

to his full height, he let out a heaving sigh and cast a long look at Werner, finally nodding his reluctant agreement.

"I'll go as far as Solomon's and no further, Werner," he finally spoke, the firmness in his voice offering no question as to his sincerity.

"Thank you, Jakob," offered the other.

The two boys had been on the hunt for three hours now. In the town of Wertzenberg, the Green Woodpecker was something of a local legend. The older townsfolk used to entertain the boys with tales of sightings from years gone by - a splendid bird, its plumes as green as the most exotic fern, its crown a stunning crimson. As the tales went on, the boys had formed a fascination with the bird and their outings in the woods took on a new flair; the games of pirates or warlord now took on an added twist. Their young lives, lazy and carefree, had purpose it seemed, and they vowed they would find the bird.

Every young boy needs a myth to chase.

And so it was, the two friends pressed onward, deep into the woods outside of Wertzenberg. Far into the woods, they chased their dream.

Werner set off first, pointing his improvised walking stick far off into the woods, the direction of Solomon's place. The younger boy picked up his stick and followed, matching his gait to the other's, the faint chattering of the woodpecker far off in the distance.

Solomon's place was something of a myth in its own right. Deep in the woods, well beyond where anyone would think someone might live, was a stone house that had stood for years. All of the local boys who adventured in these woods knew of the place and avoided it. How and why someone would live so deep in these woods was a mystery to all, including the adults in town.

Werner and Jakob had only seen him once. He was tall and gangly, the frame and face of a very old man, hunched over and shuffling slowly along a pathway near the house, his eyes covered by the shadow of a wide brimmed hat. He never once looked at them, but they knew he saw them as they huddled behind a woodpile some distance in the woods. The local boys had dubbed him Solomon after "Solomon Grundy", the zombie of lore and that's how he was thereafter known. The boys generally left the strange man alone; his house was spooky and foreboding and even boys with dreams and myths to chase tended to give it a wide berth.

For another half hour, the two boys pressed onwards, following the chattering and clacking sounds of the woodpecker. They had heard the noises before and had rushed off in excitement, only to find they had gone the wrong way. The woods were sneaky and often played games with sounds, bouncing them from tree to tree and sending the boys off on wild chases. This day, however, the sounds seemed consistent and clear, a steady clicking and the occasional clacking.

Click, click, click, click, click, clack...

And so it went, the rapid clicking continued. Somewhere deep in the woods, somewhere near Solomon's place, was the Green Woodpecker, and they would find it this day.

The sun settled at eye level, well below the crest of the trees. Werner knew they had little time and he gestured for Jakob to hurry as the younger boy had fallen behind, clearly exhausted.

Up ahead rose the high, crumbling slate roof of Solomon's. In the fading light of the forest, the unnatural square shape of the house could be seen from some distance. The trunks of the trees stood like black matchsticks as dusk fell over the woods. A sudden chill ran Werner's spine as they approached.

Click, click, click, click, click, clack…

It was much louder now, the Green Woodpecker, straight ahead. It must have found sanctuary at Solomon's house, perhaps chipping holes into the old rotting wood sides of the crumbling house.

Werner turned to the younger boy and smiled, a long, quiet smile, his face full of excitement at the end of their epic quest. Jakob smiled back, and they shared a moment. Two adventurers, two kindred spirits, once pirates, then warriors, now, famed ornithologists, who had found the legendary Green Woodpecker.

It was just ahead, the source of the sound. The boys moved closer so as not to spook it. Slowly, carefully, they picked their way through the dense shrubbery that bordered the property. Just over there, on the far side of the house, Werner was sure of it.

They moved along gingerly, picking softly through the bushes until they had almost reached a clearing where they would get a good view of the bird in action.

Click, click, click, click, click, clack...

Much, much louder now.

Their hearts raced in anticipation as the quickly-setting sun pushed them onwards to get a glimpse of the emerald breast of the bird before the sun set.

They gave one last look at each other, the last time their lives would be normal and mundane, the last time they would be unknown adventurers. Everyone in Wertzenberg would know their names - Werner and Jakob of the great expedition. It was what boyhood dreams were all about.

Werner pushed through the undergrowth first. The smaller boy behind him eagerly brushed his cheek past Werner's shoulder to get a glimpse, as well. The last few branches fell away, and the boys emerged into the clearing, staring in awe at the source of the sound.

And the source of the sound looked back at them with wild red eyes that bore straight through them. Squatting on the back porch of Solomon's decrepit house with black, scaly skin, gangly limbs and grotesque fingers tipped with razor-sharp claws, the creature cocked its head and turned its gaze to the woods.

Click, click, click, click, clack… came the sound as its hideous mouth with row after row of sharpened teeth moved quickly, gnawing on something in its grip. Its teeth gnashed violently against each other as it shredded some unknown meal.

The boys stumbled forward, their momentum pushing them a few steps into the clearing. The creature dropped what it had been devouring and fixed its gaze on them. Werner couldn't help but let his eyes follow the creature's meal as it fell to the porch.

It seemed impossible and took a moment to register as his mind clearly wished to think otherwise, but there was no doubt what he saw - a human arm, or at least the remnants of one, a bloody stump on one end and a curled, withered hand on the other. The severed limb dropped unceremoniously down to the hard wood next to what was left of a human body - an old human body.

Solomon's body.

A blur of black and red flew past Werner.

THE GREEN WOODPECKER

In his subconscious, Werner thought that Jakob's scream was muffled, almost as if he was sleeping and someone awake in the distance was howling. The shrieking death throes of the young boy were merely background noise as Werner's mind reeled to absorb what it had just seen, not enough capacity to take in the sounds of his friend's blood curdling cries.

And with that, Werner's young mind shut down and went black. His last image was of the Green Woodpecker, perched high on the roof. Its emerald breast and red crown stood brilliantly against the fading sun.

Click, click, click, click, clack...

A
GRAVE
MISTAKE

A GRAVE MISTAKE

The brusque sounds pierced through the intangible blackness that consumed her - a sharp thud followed by the sound of scraping across rough wood and then a momentary silence. The world was quiet for one second, then two, then the thud-scrape once more.

The steady, measured sounds stirred her mind with the rhythms of life and beckoned her from faltering grips of unconsciousness.

Thud.

Scrape.

Silence.

In her brain, the neurons fired valiantly, clawing and scrambling to dredge life from the precipice of death.

Thud.

Scrape.

Silence.

Her eyelids twitched and spasmed violently like two curtains rippling against a tremendous storm. Her hands began to vibrate, sending shivers down the length of her body.

Thud.

Scrape.

Her eyelids shot open and her eyes bulged from her head. Her chest sunk deep and her mouth gaped like the desperate catch of some grizzled fisherman, gasping hard for air. She sucked in the warm air and pushed it out again, her chest heaving uncontrollably for several long, deep breaths.

Her whole body quivered with the breaths until finally she settled, her lungs having filled themselves with precious oxygen. She pressed her hands to her side and raised herself only a few inches before the crown of her head banged hard against wood. She fell onto her back, noticing the strange contour of quilted silk beneath her. Curling her fingers, she felt around her, her hands running over satiny cushions dotted with fat, upholstered buttons.

A GRAVE MISTAKE

In the blackness, she looked towards her feet and saw nothing. She lifted her legs and felt her dress glide and flow with her movements like a gentle ocean wave crashing around a familiar, rounded rock. After only inches, her bare toes bumped into wood, firm and unforgiving.

She lay back and closed her eyes, resting her head on a thick, silken pillow, her soft brown hair falling to either side. Her mind swirled in desperate circles, seeking some foothold of reality upon which to rest. She opened her eyes once more and reached up with her hands, pressing her palms against the hard wood.

She could feel the air around her growing warmer. The sweat began to bead on her forehead and rolled sideways along her temple until it soaked into her delicate hair. She could feel her chest begin to rise and fall rapidly as the panic coursed through her body. Closing her eyes, she focused as best as she could, inhaling measured breaths through her nose and letting it fall from her mouth.

Once again, she opened her eyes and strained to look around her but saw nothing – only the dead blackness. She lifted her arms and slid her fingers along the wooded ceiling until she found the edges. Her long nails made a gentle scraping noise as she traced around her vainly for some escape. She found nothing.

The air grew hot and moist and her eyes began to water from the condensation. Her lungs began to fill with warm, stale air and her throat grew dry and constricted.

Her chest heaved erratically, and tears pooled in the corners of her eyes as she began to sob. Her body bounced rhythmically off the satin cushions to the cadence of her grief.

In the depths of sorrow, her mind reached deep into its memories and began to play images through her head.

Across the table, he gazed at her lovingly. In the flickering light of the candle, his eyes sparkled a deep, seafoam green and seemed to soak into her heart. He smiled at her and slid his hand across the snow white table cloth and took her hand in his. Around them, hushed voices of joyful conversations mingled with the soft-stringed melodies of some unseen violinist. She smiled at him, her red lips stretching wide around her teeth, and then looked down coyly.

"I love you, Veronica," he said, the words coming smoothly from his mouth.

A GRAVE MISTAKE

She knew he did.

"I love you, Eric," she replied after a calculated pause, lifting her chin to meet his eyes.

For a moment, their gaze locked on each other and their spirits mingled from across the table. The flame of the candle curved and bent, its light bouncing and reflecting from the sharp crystal edges of the chandelier above them. The lights sparkled and danced, a hue of brilliant colors rushing into her eye. Suddenly, her smile faded and her mouth dropped open. Her hand went limp, falling to the white cloth with a thud. Her eyes rolled back in her head, the black pupils disappearing beneath her eyelids. She slumped back in her seat and began to seize, her body quaking violently. And then her world faded to black.

The warmth of the tears streaming down her cheeks brought her back to the present. She opened her eyes once more and looked around. Her eyes had adjusted to the darkness and she could now make out faint shapes in the dark. As she craned her neck downward, she could see the outline of her bare feet, her toes just inches from the hard, wooden ceiling of the coffin. She scanned the darkness, searching vainly for some means of escape but found none. All around her, an impenetrable wooden casket sealed her from the outside world.

The air around was hot and moist, like a wall of humidity on a southern, summer day. Her breaths came fast and labored now as she consumed the last vestiges of oxygen in desperate, gasping breaths. In a fit of panic, she thrashed about, kicking her feet and pounding her hands on the lid of the coffin. She bludgeoned the thick wood with her tiny fists until they throbbed. The nails on her toes cracked and bent as her feet smashed upward. The wood stared back at her indifferently in the hot blackness.

She collapsed motionless onto the silk cushions and gasped, her chest wheezing and sucking at the vacuum around her. Her racing mind began to slow, the thoughts now churning slowly through an encroaching fog of shadows. Her breathing slowed as faint puffs of air expelled through her lips. The rising and falling of her chest was barely perceptible in the blackness.

As the haze of death drew its sullen shroud around her, she closed her eyes and welcomed the merciful blackness.

THE VIGIL OVER SAINT AGNES

CHAPTER ONE

The ticking of the clock was interminable.

For three days, Hutchens sat in the worn, reclining chair keeping vigil over the old man. On the wall above the bed, the black metal hands of the ancient round clock droned the dead rhythm of endless time.

Every night, the old man tossed and turned in his bed. His tortured movements punctuated mercifully by momentary pauses of sleep.

In the darkness, Hutchens had little to do. Perpetually, he counted the scarce minutes of sleep that had befallen him these last several days. To his best count, he had slept five hours in three nights, his only solace coming when the old man had finally found a restful position. Hutchens was conditioned now. The shallow snoring from the darkened bed signaled him to close his eyes and slumber. Yet just as he began to doze, the old man would toss and turn. His clawing at the bedframe or the soft thud of a pillow hitting the lacquered floor would startle Hutchens awake to begin the process anew.

Four days ago, the old man had cramped over with pains in his abdomen, retching at the wooden table. His eyes bulged, and he doubled in pain. Hutchens had called for the ambulance and two soulless attendants had whisked the old man to this the stoic, gray hospital.

Ever since, he lay in the bed, the maze of tubes and devices stringing him to the metal bedframe like some sickly marionette. Occasionally, a hollow-eyed doctor or some frowning nurse would visit the room and perform a perfunctory check on the old man. For the most part, Hutchens had borne the burden of his care, shifting pillows and blankets when the man was restless and holding the crooked handle of the urinal when the man beckoned in his labored breaths.

THE VIGIL OVER SAINT AGNES

Now, the old man's shallowed snores rose softly above the bed. Hutchens leaned back in the chair hesitantly, well-knowing that he would soon be needed at the bedside. Behind him, a storm engulfed the old hospital like some hungry snake consuming a rotten carcass. Thunder clapped outside the window and lines of rain splashed across the thick windowpanes. Sporadically, streaks of lightning would arc through the sky, turning the blackness of the hospital room into the backlit stage of some somber medical drama.

Hutchens pushed gently on the leg rest with his calves and sat upright in the chair. The old man snored almost melodically before him. Sleep beckoned Hutchens desperately from the depths of his mind, yet the storm called him to the window. His weary soul craved life outside these grim walls in all of its splashing and crackling. He rose from the chair and paced softly to the window, cautious not to wake the old man.

He stood before the thick panes of glass and gazed into the black night. His puffed eyes stung as he strained to form images beyond the windowpane. Long threads of water arced into the glass before him and rolled in great beads down to the cobbled sill.

In the distance, Hutchens could see the North wing of the hospital, its gray-black wall jutting out into the courtyard like the buttress on some medieval castle. A dozen windows dotted the cold stone wall in bland and predictable intervals.

A streak of lightning lit the sky and Hutchens stepped back from the window instinctively, the white light startling him. In the flash of light, the windows of the North wing reflected back the South wing, like two lifeless tombs signaling their existence to the other.

Hutchens looked down to the ground some ten stories below. In the darkness, the lush green grass of the courtyard looked like the cloak of some black specter laid out between the two wings of the hospital.

Behind him, the sounds of the old man stirring filled Hutchens' ears, his mind now painfully conditioned to the slightest movement. He started to turn back towards the bed as a flash of lightning streaked vertically through the sky just above the North wing. Hutchens gasped suddenly, and a jolt of adrenaline coursed through his body, repelling his fatigue.

Hutchens was sure he had seen something

perched on the roof of the North wing, illuminated by the crack of lightning. His mind was dull and faltering from sleep deprivation, but he was positive there had been something there – something black and leathery, with sinewy limbs and bat-like wings, perched high on the old hospital.

He stepped back from the window and struggled to control his breathing. His chest rose and fell from the unexpected fright as he stared up at the edge of the hospital waiting for the lightning to flash again. The rain licked at the window filling the room with the sounds of a rushing stream gliding across the glass panes. Suddenly, the skies flashed again, and the shadowy courtyard became a harsh white for a split second. Hutchens darted his eyes to the ledge of the North wing for a sight of the creature. Atop the old stone building, there was nothing at all.

He walked backwards from the window, his mind struggling to come to terms with what he had seen. His hands rose to his face and his fingers pressed into the corners of his eyes near the bridge of his nose as if the pressure would somehow reset his consciousness. Walking slowly across the room, he lowered himself into the reclining chair and his body sagged into the soft leather.

Hutchens leaned back in the chair and closed his eyes. The old man's soft snoring filled the small room, muting the rain and soft thunder beyond the window. The alluring call of sleep convinced him he was imagining things and soon he drifted into a deep slumber.

CHAPTER TWO

T he bitter lightning cracked outside the window, almost vengeful that Hutchens had dared close his eyes. The electrified zip-snap reverberated in his ears like an old tin roof shaken asunder. He lurched forward in his chair subconsciously, moving away from the window.

Before him, the old man's snores trailed off into a heavy puffing, the breaths pressing their way haphazardly from his nostrils, threatening to wake him from his slumber. Hutchens held his breath. He could feel the sweat beading on his forehead. He stared in silence at the old man, daring not move lest he wake and begin to thrash in his bed once more.

The rain pelted the windowpanes now, the fat droplets playing a steady cadence on the thick glass. Hutchens turned and looked over his shoulder out the window and into the blackness of the night. He rose to his feet and his mind replayed the creature he swore he had seen on the crest of the North wing scant hours before.

In the silence, he stood motionless, willing the old man back into his dormant trance. In the darkness, Hutchens could see the hands on the clock – they read 3:24AM. He resolved to leave the room and stretch his legs in the long hallways of the blackened hospital. When the old man's rough snore began once more, Hutchens stepped gently towards the door and out into the hallway.

As he stepped from the room, his eyes cast down the long corridor. A dozen wooden doors lined the shadowy hallway on either side like stoic soldiers in some somber parade. To the right, fifty paces ahead, the dim lights of the nurse's station flickered vainly against the shadows.

A gaunt face turned slowly towards Hutchens from the desk, her jet-black hair fell to either side of her pale, angular face. She stared at him for a long moment with dead eyes and said nothing. Her gaze bore through him as if asking why he dared venture into the hallway.

"Do you need something?" said the nurse, her tone as sterile and cold as the hospital itself.

"Just stretching my legs," sputtered Hutchens nervously. She looked back at him for a moment and then, without a word, turned her head back down to the desk. A shudder ran down Hutchens' spine and he turned and headed in the other direction down the hallway.

Since 1871, Saint Agnes Hospital had loomed over the sleepy town of Somerville. The drab, gray monolith had been constructed with granite and limestone from the nearby quarry, dragged on wooden sleds by bent-back mules and teams of horses. For over two centuries, the hospital had risen from the hillside just outside the town as a beacon of prosperity and civility. Following the Civil War, families migrated west to this fertile valley and began to establish homesteads. As the population grew, the need for a hospital became quickly apparent and Saint Agnes rose majestically from the foothills to serve the needs of the burgeoning community.

Hutchens had never been in the hospital before. In fact, he'd only visited this area occasionally whenever the old man ailed from something that required his visit. As he stepped slowly down the darkened hallway, he mused at the gloom of the place. For a hospital that had birthed countless children and saved the lives of thousands in this area, the place exuded an unmistakably dark aura.

He moved along quietly, passing the thick, wooden doors on either side, closed tight as if guarding their secrets. At the end of the hallway was a dim light, faintly illuminating the elevator vestibule. Hutchens walked to the pair of old elevators and pressed the bottom button. On the way in, he had seen a covered patio that would protect him from the rain yet allow him to temporarily escape the suffocating confines of this bleak place.

The old metal cables growled and moaned as they called the elevator forth from the depths of the building. When they stopped, the two doors vibrated as if trying to open, then paused and finally, they drew open. Hutchens stepped into the elevator, his shoes treading lightly on the dark checkered wood floor. In the faint light, he reached forward and pressed the lowest button. The doors rattled briefly again, then closed and he began his descent.

After a moment the iron cable ceased grinding and the elevator came to a rest, bouncing gently. Once more, the doors hesitated as if questioning whether they should open and then spread apart, greeting Hutchens with another blackened hallway. He stepped out of the elevator tentatively. Although he admittedly had spent scant time on the first floor of the hospital, this place seemed deeply unfamiliar.

He looked around. On one side, the hallway ended into a cold, concrete wall. On the other, it bent sharply to the left just a few feet away, the glow of a faint light guiding the path. Hutchens looked straight ahead from the elevator opening and squinted his eyes to read the faded metal sign.

"BASEMENT," it read. He'd gone too far.

As he turned back towards the elevator, the doors closed swiftly and smoothly, without hesitation. The old metal cable began to grind once more, wearily pulling the elevator upwards.

Hutchens thrust his hand towards the button and then stopped, his finger hesitating over the arrow. He withdrew his hand and started around the bend in the hallway.

Turning the corner past the elevators, the hallway stretched before him portentously. The sounds of industrial machines and the rushing of pipes filled the cavernous space. At the far end, a pale square formed on the floor, drawn by some bright light emanating from a side room. Hutchens started forward towards the light, the monotony of his vigil over the old man driving him forward with curiosity.

As he approached the light, the noises grew louder. He could hear the sounds of hungry machines going about their tasks. Their engines and belts churned heavily in the catacomb of the basement. As he drew closer to the doorway, the distinctive smell of laundry filled his nostrils – heavy starches, industrial soaps, and the faint smell of lint heating in a dryer. Hutchens stood next to a metal cart just beside the open doorway for a moment gathering himself and then slowly poked his head around the corner.

The vast room was painted a dull white, the concrete walls dotted with iron-gray pipes and vents jutting haphazardly all about. Rows of giant machines lined the walls – washers, dryers, and steam machines of some sort. Beyond the tall, rigid laundry racks, Hutchens saw movement. He strained his tired eyes to see through the starched white gowns and blankets hanging like limp ghosts and could make out a tall, bald-headed man in a dark orderly's uniform working in the distance. The man stood over a gurney and worked with long bony fingers, stripping a blood-soaked sheet from the thin mattress. Hutchens gasped in horror at the sight. He had seen his share of blood before, but this was something completely different; the native white of the sheet barely visible through the sickly, sanguine stains.

Hutchens stepped back awkwardly, his foot landing on the bottom rail of the metal cart. He waved his arms frantically to regain his balance. The old, iron wheel of the cart rose and then fell to the ground, clattering loudly on the unforgiving concrete. Inside the laundry room, the orderly turned mechanically at the sound, his vision knifing skillfully through the hanging gowns and sheets and landing directly on Hutchens. His coal-black eyes rested deep within bony sockets and his sharp cheeks rose dramatically, giving him an almost skeletal appearance.

Hutchens turned in the darkness and fled back towards the elevator. His rubber soled shoes pounded on the concrete and he flailed his finger towards the elevator call button. His heart raced as the old, iron cable spun, lowering the elevator car slowly to the basement. Once more, the doors shuddered and then opened and Hutchens lurched inside, thrashing madly at the vertical row of buttons. The doors inched closed and he sagged against the wall and exhaled deeply, his heart racing.

The old elevator creaked and groaned its melancholy journey to the ninth floor, marking its arrival with a sudden bucking as the cable stopped unceremoniously and the metal chute came to rest. The doors bumped together once and then opened. The long, black hallway loomed ahead of Hutchens like the endless maw of some black serpent.

He stepped gingerly off the elevator. His ears pulsed with the gentle heaving of his chest as the breath sucked and gasped from him in frightened, staccato patterns. At the end of the hall, he saw the familiar, dim light of the nurse's station lighting a faint circular patch on the checkered floor.

Hutchens gathered himself and stepped quickly towards the old man's room, his mind attuned to the deathly quiet behind him, waiting for the sounds of the old cable to grind to the basement and retrieve the grim orderly. But there was only silence.

As he approached the door to the old man's room, the nurse raised her head slowly from the desk and turned towards him, her motions cold and rigid. Her sunken eyes bored into him again. He could literally feel her gaze staring beyond his outer flesh, penetrating somewhere deep into his frightened core. He looked away and said nothing, moving quickly through the door into the old man's room.

The oblivious snores from the hospital bed said nothing of what Hutchens had seen. As far as the old man was concerned, Hutchens had never left the comfort of the reclining chair.

Hutchens glanced down at the old man. The tranquility of his deep slumber was calming to observe. If the old man could sleep so carelessly in this dreadful place, it must be quite alright, he tried to convince himself.

Outside, the lightning flashed, reflecting the beads of water on the window. The rain had subsided now, and the water came only in a light mist. Even the lightning was tame now, the brief flash scarcely recognizable in comparison to the frenzied bolts from earlier in the night. Hutchens stepped to the window and looked out once more, his eyes casting upwards towards the roof of the North wing. The lightning flashed again - gentle and voiceless. On the roof of the North wing, there was nothing at all.

Hutchens turned back towards the old man and slid his lean frame into the reclining chair. His mind began to relax. *Sleep deprivation is a hell of a thing*, he thought. He pulled the lever on the side of the recliner, stretching the leg rest forward. Leaning back, he closed his eyes and soon, the sleep engulfed him.

CHAPTER THREE

T he ticking of the old, round clock droned in his ears, setting cadence to his slumber.

Tick, tick, tick, tick...

In the blackness of unconsciousness, he could see the clock's hands circling like some black, tin soldier condemned to an endless march. His eyes twitched behind their eyelids and his hands trembled softly, buried in some half-dream.

In his dream, he felt a soft needle prick in his right hand. A cool liquid coursed up his arm, traveling his veiny channels and spreading out across his chest. Suddenly, his eyes flashed open and a burning sensation rippled through him as his chest pumped the liquid through his body. He opened his mouth to scream but could only gasp, the words caught in the bone-dry chasm of his constricted throat.

In the darkness above him, he could see the outline of a face staring down at him. Her hollow eyes absorbed his silent terror and reflected it back as a palette of nothingness. He clutched at the armrest in his mind, struggling to move but his fingers and arm were frozen, unresponsive to his mind's commands.

The nurse turned her head sideways and cast her gaze upon the old man. Hutchens could hear the deep thrumming of his snoring. In the doorway, a shadow loomed, stretching to the ceiling as it approached and entered the room. He could hear the squeaking of wheels but was unable to turn his head to see the source. The shadow drew near, and Hutchens could just make out his form beyond the nurse's dispassionate gaze.

In the dim corner of the room, barely lit by the glow from the hallway, the orderly appeared, pushing an old gurney whose iron wheels cried a shrill, unwelcome greeting. The orderly turned towards Hutchens, his sharp features looking like a hatchet in the blackness of the room.

"Don't worry," said the nurse, her voice barely above a rasp. "We'll take good care of him," she said, casting a short glance towards the old man. Behind her, the orderly stood motionless, like some lifeless cadaver.

They lifted Hutchens onto the gurney. In his mind, he fought valiantly, struggling and clawing against the two. In reality, his body lay frozen and motionless and they lifted him from the recliner like a dried board and strapped him into the gurney. Hutchens stared into the ceiling, eyes agape. The cracks and ridges on the old ceiling tile began to pass slowly as they wheeled the gurney from the room and into the dark hall.

After a moment, he heard the familiar grinding of the old, iron cable as the obedient elevator rose once more. The wheels squeaked as the gurney moved into the chute and the doors closed behind. From the periphery of his vision, Hutchens could see the nebulous form of their two shadows in the corners of the elevator.

The faltering doors buckled once and then

closed. In the elevator, the air grew stale and dead. Hutchens' frozen eyes stared at the bland, wooden tiles on the elevator ceiling. The lights seemed to flicker and dim and once again, the old, iron cable began to grind its weary hymn, and the elevator started to rise.

Every cell in Hutchens' body screamed in terror but his voice was mute, unable to conjure as much as a whimper. His eyes flickered from left to right desperately, as if unleashing the movements the rest of his body failed to muster.

The old elevator creaked and groaned a short distance and then the doors shuddered once more, bumping together as if summoning the will to open and then spread apart. The two figures approached from either side of the stretcher – the nurse on his right and the orderly on his left. In the erratic twitching of his eyes, Hutchens barely notice them exchange a somber, almost frightened glance, and then they each grasped the gurney and it began to roll once more.

Above him, the brown tiles of the elevator ceiling faded beyond the elevator threshold and melded into the dull, white panels of the hospital hallway, cloaked in a shadowy mist. The wheels of the gurney rolled with purpose now, as if the grim attendants wished to expedite their task.

Hutchens strained his eyes towards his feet now and peered over the tips of his leather shoes. The orderly's gaunt, withered arm reached forward and pulled on the thick, outer door. Suddenly, a cool blanket of wind drew over Hutchens, his skin tingling as the stale hospital air gave way to the chill of the black night. He felt the gurney bump and roll over a threshold and then his whole body was shrouded in the night sky. Above him, a gentle rain fell across his body, barely more than a fine mist. He could feel every tiny droplet landing on him like moist pinpricks and blinked rapidly as a thin film of water formed on his eyes.

His mind flashed for a moment to the angry storm from earlier with the lashing rain and the fierce lightning. For a split second, his subconscious wandered from his predicament and embraced the gentle aftermath of the storm. But the hurried grinding of the gurney wheels on rough concrete snapped him back to the present.

"Here," said the nurse to the orderly in her dead tone, calling them to a halt.

The wheels of the gurney stopped abruptly, and Hutchens' body slid slightly forward and stopped at the tug of his restraints. There was a palpable sense of foreboding emanating from the nurse and the orderly. Their previously stoic nature had given way to a tangible sense of disquiet. Hutchens twisted his eyes as far as they could go to the left and looked at the orderly. His lean, skeletal figure was hunched now, as if cowering from something unseen. His bony fingers worked feverishly to unstrap the restraints that bound Hutchens to the gurney.

What were they doing? Why had they brought him here?

"Hurry!" hissed the nurse from his right. Hutchens' eyes flickered towards her and watched her step backward, her once-dead eyes suddenly alive with a visible dread. The orderly fumbled about hastily and then turned and scurried from view. Hutchens felt the pressure of the restraints release as they fell to the side of the gurney with a dull flap.

In his mind, he summoned every ounce of his will to sit upright. His brain conjured images of him sitting up and then rolling off the gurney as if he could somehow create reality through his imagination. But his body would not obey, and he lay motionless in the cool night sky as the beads of water formed around his blanched face.

High above, the half-moon hung solemnly, as if hiding a secret beyond the penumbra. The soft wind whistled across the rooftop, the gentle breeze rippling the legs of Hutchens' cotton pants in tiny waves of fabric.

Thwump. Thwump.

The gentle breeze of the black night gave way to short, powerful bursts of wind. Hutchens' ears filled with the pounding of great wings flapping and the natural hum of the night seemed to recede before the ominous sound.

Thwump. Thwump.

The forceful rhythm of the wings grew closer now as if hidden just beyond the shadows of his vision. Hutchens strained his eyes downward toward his feet, desperate for the source of the noise. The gusts of wind blew across him from feet to head, tousling his chestnut hair and fanning the beads of water from his face.

From beyond his feet, he could feel a presence as if the air bristled and moved in repulsion from its form. Unbridled panic spread through his body like an electrical charge. His sternum pounded visibly as his heart pumped violently below. Hutchens fought desperately once more with his mind to regain control of his body yet again, but his will was beaten back by the drugs that coursed through his veins.

Then, before him it appeared, emerging from the shadows like some ungodly abomination. Broad, leathery wings laced with pulsing veins stretched beyond his field of vision on either side, shining like slick onyx in the dim moonlight. Hutchens' forehead wretched upward in terror, his bulbous eyes stark white against the blackness of the night. From the end of the gurney, a pair of deep ruby eyes glowed back at him, set above a gaping maw of razor teeth the size of daggers. The eyes burned like molten lava swirling around two, tiny black pupils that fixated horribly on his helpless form.

Thwump. Thwump.

On its great black wings, the creature hovered effortlessly in the caliginous night and then drew near. The wicked, curved talons of its hands stretched wide and its mouth opened into a pale void set with jagged fangs.

THE VIGIL OVER SAINT AGNES

The pulsing of the creature's sinewy wings blew a soft gale across Hutchens and cleared the mist from his eyes, his nightmare no longer shrouded behind the thin layer of water. The creature beat its great wings once more and then set upon him. Its dagger fangs tore into the flesh of his chest, ripping open his sternum and exposing his innards to the black night. Hutchens screamed horribly in his mind, yet the night was deathly silent beyond the ravenous feasting of the creature high on the roof of Saint Agnes.

GHOSTS
OF THE ROAD

GHOSTS OF THE ROAD

The plastic vent cover rattled quietly with each disturbance of the road, its steady, inanimate chattering resonating in the stillness of the vehicle. At first, it had been a nuisance but as the miles passed, the rattling had become something of a comfort - a lifeless companion in the otherwise hollow car barreling down the black, frigid, Iowa highway.

Newman had been at the wheel for eleven hours now, a journey that had begun in eastern Ohio and which now carried him westwards towards Nebraska. The temperature gauge on the dashboard registered two degrees below zero. The thought of the frosty chill outside brought a deeper solitude to the February night.

On the dashboard, the faded, digital numbers of the vehicle clock shone a time of 2:03AM. The number "3" looked derelict and unfulfilled, missing a single, vertical dash in its composition.

Frozen, dark farmland stretched across the shallow horizon in either direction. The white lights of Newman's sedan stretched vainly off to each side of the highway, illuminating the near edges of the fields on either side. The passing headlights briefly shone on the greenish-brown of the Iowa countryside that blurred unceremoniously into the black concrete in a droning hypnosis. Aside from the occasional tractor trailer barreling determinedly to some unknown destination, he was alone.

Newman leaned forward in his leather seat, twisting at the aches and knots formed from hours hunched over the steering wheel as a deep yawn emanated outwards. His mouth stretched wide and his eyes squeezed tight. Omaha was three more hours ahead and it was only seven hours until he'd be behind his table at the convention hall masking his misery behind a lifeless smile. His bleary eyes were sure to betray his normally energetic salesmanship.

Tugging at the collar of his stiff polo shirt, he calculated the short sleep that lay ahead once he reached the hotel. He reached out and turned on the radio. The soothing sound of soft static filled the car's cabin as his hand ran through a crown of stringy hair. His spirits lifted slightly, and a small token of energy permeated his weary frame as the crackling of the radio broached the silence and provided a temporary companion of sorts. Reaching out slightly, he pressed the scan button to the right in search of a station.

In a moment, the crackling ceased and the radio fell silent, save an almost imperceptible hiss. Newman moved his hand away tentatively, offering a moment for the connection to manifest.

At first the voice was faint, but something wakened deep inside him. The tone, the mannerisms were so distant but familiar. He leaned his ear towards the dashboard, straining to focus between the gentle hiss of the radio and the suddenly tedious rattle of the car vent.

"Peter..."

He was sure he had heard it– his name rasped in the faint hush of an old woman's voice.

"Peter... where... are... you... going...?" it said. The voice was familiar and kind, but the words were stretched thin with concern and something that registered as despair.

Newman sat back quickly in the seat, sliding himself so he was completely upright. He intentionally widened his eyes and focused firmly on the road ahead. The dark fields flashed by on either side of the vehicle in anonymity.

"Be careful, Peter…" whispered the voice on the radio. This time, the voice carried a strange mix of compassion and an almost sinister mocking.

Newman focused for a moment, the words resonating in his mind. The voice was unmistakable now. He was sure it was his grandmother, Margaret, dead for a decade and long since buried in eastern Ohio.

Fumbling clumsily for the bottled water in the center console, Newman spun the cap off with one hand. The white plastic top spun down the side of his leg into the abyss between the seats. He swigged hard at the bottle, finishing the remnants of the lukewarm water and pressed the scan button on the radio with a sense of urgency.

Straightening both arms on the wheel, he arched his back and shook himself out of the fog. Eight hours behind him and just three more to go before his head hit the motel pillow for a well-earned slumber. *No dozing off at the wheel*, he told himself. Newman pushed the voice from his head and firmed his resolve for the final push towards Nebraska.

The pavement moved under his car hypnotically, black asphalt and yellow lines endlessly cycling as if wound around some invisible wheel. He glanced down at the clock on the dashboard. The faded, emerald "3" now reflected a broken "8" as the time registered 2:08AM.

The momentary crackling of the radio between channels suddenly fell to silence as a new station registered a connection.

"I'm sorry…" spoke a man's voice, faint but firmly.

Newman perked up, excited at the prospect of a late-night radio talk show.

"I tried to save you…" whispered the man's voice, this time sounding strained with emotion, almost ghastly in tone.

Newman's brow furrowed. The voice whistled through his subconscious, searching for a match. After a second, his shoulders shuddered as he recognized the voice on the radio as his best friend, Thomas — two years dead from a boating accident on Lake George.

Newman's index finger lurched forward suddenly. He poked hard at the power button for the radio, shutting down the lighted console. The darkness engulfed the driver's cabin, the faint green glow of the broken clock the only beacon in the darkened chamber.

Newman realized that he wasn't going to make Omaha with the specter of sleep overcoming him and his mind tangled in the tricks of the road. He had no choice but to stop, and began scanning the road signs for some sort of rest stop or gas station.

A mile passed and then two and three. In the distance, Newman could make out the deep green of the highway sign, the logo of the commercial gas station harkened back into the cold night like a friendly beacon. The exit was just a mile ahead.

"You almost made it..." came the sound of his own voice suddenly from the speaker.

His eyes flashed open in terror as the lights of the radio flickered on. The entire dashboard brightened and the broken bar on the digital clock character suddenly filled in with a sharp green hue. The glowing digits were suddenly full and alive, their vibrant green casting a harsh glow on his sweat-mottled face.

Newman's hands trembled at the wheel, his muscles twitched and his vision flickered violently between the haze of blurred pavement, the sudden sharpness of the digital console, and the dirty brown-green of the Iowa fields whipping by in swaths of headlights. Suddenly, he felt the tail of the car quiver and slip on a patch of ice. His hands clutched frantically at the steering wheel in a desperate overcorrection.

On the cold, desolate highway, the sedan turned harshly. The tail-end slipped and lifted, and the car began to roll, spinning violently like a halogen-lit cyclone into the bleak and lonely fields.

A dusty cloud settled around the wrecked shell of the vehicle. The wintry Iowa silence was disturbed only by a brisk February wind against the tall, dry grass and the fading static of a broken radio.

THE BEAST WITHIN

CHAPTER ONE

The full moon hung solemnly over the arid fields like a watchful eye, gazing dispassionately at the world below. Long shadows drifted over the landscape, the wispy clouds casting patches of drifting darkness across the valley. Gilbert Fogg watched anxiously from the open windows of his disheveled wooden shack, his ears tuned to the sounds of the autumn night.

"Gilbert. Come to bed, love," gently pleaded his wife Margaret, the soft lilt of her voice riding melodically in the stillness of the room.

Gilbert paused briefly at the window and then drew the shutters closed, fastening them carefully with an iron buckle. Shuffling across the wooden planks, he sat slowly on the edge of the bed, still listening for something.

"It's only a matter of time..." he muttered, his gravelly voice trailing off as he lifted his legs onto the bed and slid himself next to Margaret's warm body.

Before long, the darkness of sleep engulfed them, and they fell into a deep slumber as the cloak of blackness fell upon them.

Almost before the first shrill cries pierced the quiet night, Gilbert was awake. He sat straight up in the bed and his spine stiffened with a powerful mixture of adrenaline and fear. Somewhere in the darkness, a human voice cried in agony. It shrieked like a man whose spirit and composure were being torn asunder, leaving nothing but the most hopeless and desperate primal howls.

Margaret rolled towards Gilbert, resting her hand on his leg, gripping him tightly with her bony fingers. Instinctively, he clutched her hand in his and grasped firmly, both of them staring blindly into the darkness. The wails of the dying man resounded through the valley as they sat motionless and listened.

And then they were no more. The cacophonous throes of mortal terror fell silent and once more the night was still.

After several minutes, Gilbert lay back on the bed, his forehead glistening with the pallor of cold sweat. His breathing was deep and labored. Margaret soothed him as best as she could, but for the remainder of the night, Gilbert lay awake, his eyes fixed on the ceiling, his mind echoing with the sounds of human agony.

As morning broke in the small hamlet of Drendel, the peasants were active. While some had returned to their fields to tend their crops, a large number had gathered at the foot of the gently sloping hill that lead to the estate of Lord Chambliss, the man who owned these lands and for whom they were employed as serfs. Chambliss was a pious Lord, relatively fair with his peasants and even-handed when dealing with conflict. There was a general consensus among the group that he would at least listen to their pleas. Whether he would or could actually do something was another matter entirely, though.

As the crowd milled listlessly in the haze of morning, waiting for the presence of Chambliss, Gilbert and another man, his good friend, Nathaniel Bedford, sought different goals. Even before the sun had begun to crest on the eastern horizon, Gilbert had been at Nathaniel's door, his pitchfork in hand, rapping hard to rouse his friend.

"We must go retrieve the body, Nathaniel," he implored, knowing he would find little resistance from his dear friend. His shaggy brown hair tousled over a deep-set gaze and hawkish nose, he looked like a man who had not known amusement for many months.

Nathaniel simply nodded at his friend, reaching back for a walking stick and closed the door hurriedly behind him as his wife sat perched and somewhat bewildered on the edge of their bed. And so, the two of them had set forth into the woods that morning, as the pale rays of sun glistened weakly through the foliage of the trees above.

"If Chambliss won't listen to us, he will surely listen to the dead!" huffed Gilbert as they strode deeper and deeper into the woods.

After a considerable trek, they arrived at the

crest of a small hill, somewhere deep in the woods surrounding Erenwold. Gilbert and Nathaniel stood tall, looking carefully into the surrounding woods for the source of the noises from the night before. Several moments passed when Nathaniel called softly from the other side of the ridge.

"It's here," he said, and no other words were spoken.

Gilbert rushed to the other side of the hill and Nathaniel pointed into the foliage, perhaps fifty yards away. With a nod of acknowledgment, Gilbert started down the hill, followed by Nathaniel.

In a moment, they were knee deep in scrub brush under a canopy of trees, staring down at something before them on the ground.

"It's John Wylde," spoke Nathaniel, his thin lips curling in disgust as he uttered the words.

Gilbert again nodded. No words need be spoken.

Before them lay the body of John Wylde, fellow peasant farmer. His torso bore wicked curved slash marks, burrowing deep into his flesh and at times exposing the white hue of bone below. His face remained etched in a hideous contortion of fear and dread, and just below, nearly half of his neck lay covered in crusted blood, a series of gaping wounds giving testament to the morbid devouring of his flesh the night before.

CHAPTER TWO

A t the hill of his estate, Chambliss held court with his peasants. Still dressed in his sleeping attire, the old man had come to speak with his workers. His long silver hair disheveled against the backdrop of his verdant green lawn, he still looked the part of medieval Lord. Stroking his long beard, he looked upon the gathering of peasants still clearly frazzled by the night's events. Behind Chambliss, a small group of rough-looking men armed with pikes stood ready to ensure order among the crowd. As Lord of Erenwold, Chambliss had some freedom of action; however, in some cases, his hands were tied, and he knew not how he might help his serfs this day.

Erenwold was but one of many small hamlets comprising the kingdom of Segonius, ruled over by King Lucius of Devon. Nestled in the valley just outside Lucius' castle, Erenwold was the closest hamlet to the kingdom and Chambliss knew that he was but a stone's throw from the King's throne and consequently, the King's watchful eyes.

It had not been long since Lucius came to power, perhaps two years or more, and Chambliss, as with the other Lords who owned property within the kingdom, was still learning his way through the new bureaucracy that came with a new King. He knew little about Lucius save the fact that he often bore a wild-eyed look some said never left him after the battle of Fallonthrall when he defeated the savages to claim the region and the throne.

Lucius was an aloof King, often staying confined to his castle for weeks on end, ruling through proxies and the feudal Lords like Chambliss who served him across his Kingdom. When he did appear outside the walls of the castle though, the Lords and peasants immediately knew a King was in their presence. His tall black steed stood a head above any others in the Kingdom. His long, flowing raven hair, the sharp lines of his cheeks, his deep-set, black coal eyes, and his ever-youthful appearance, inspired an odd mix of fear, respect and devotion. Lucius had seen the wars, he had fought shoulder to shoulder with the finest men Erenwold could offer, and he had waged brutal war on the savages from the East to claim this land - his crown jewel. Despite his oddities, he had earned his crown properly and as such, his word was law.

Chambliss gazed contemplatively upon the crowd, his stomach turning knots, unknown to those before him.

As he gently shuffled his feet, preparing his words, Chambliss knew there was little he could do to appease the masses before him. He breathed deeply and began to speak, his booming tone betraying none of the worry within him.

"My people... I know why you are here..." he began.

The din of the crowd rose at his words.

"...for I, too, have heard the acts of the beast last eve," he said.

The crowd roared; a cauldron of agreement and dissention all at once.

"Against my orders, one of you saw fit to venture into the woods under the full moon!" he boomed, the directness of his words causing his stomach to turn inside.

"Give us our swords!" came a rough shout from a haggard peasant in the back as he thrust his hands high into the air. "Give us our swords!" he shouted again as others joined him, the crowd growing more restless.

"I cannot return your swords under orders from King Lucius!" shouted Chambliss, his voice taking on a fierce roar to drown out the peasants.

"You know as well as I know, that the King hath forbade the bearing of such arms by the peasants to prevent such tragedies as befell your neighbor, Peter Gage!" he bellowed, referring to an older peasant murdered some time ago over a minor drinking quarrel.

"We must defend ourselves!" cried another, his voice strained with both sorrow and desperation.

"You have your weapons, give us ours!"

growled an angry villager near the front of the crowd, leaning threateningly forward and jeering at the pikesmen behind Chambliss.

"You must remain in your homes when the moon is full as I have commanded! You should need no such weapons if your folly did not carry you out of your homes on such evenings!" reprimanded Chambliss, shouting above the crowd.

The peasants surged forward with emotion, being pushed back only by close encounters with the pikes wielded by Chambliss' men. Their grumbling and shouting grew stronger as they waved and howled, anything to gain assistance from their feudal Lord.

"John Wylde," came the punctuating shout, rising above the commotion and piercing sharply through the dull sounds of dozens of men in disunion. The crowd muffled and slowly grew quiet as Chambliss cast his gaze at a pair of men pushing through the back side of the crowd carrying a large shape wrapped in rough cloth.

Gilbert Fogg pushed forward through the parting crowd, Nathaniel at his heels, until they stood before Chambliss himself.

The body fell to the ground at Chambliss' feet with a thud as Gilbert and Nathaniel unceremoniously unfurled it from the cloth. The crowd gasped as John Wylde's mutilated body lie before then in all of his bloody glory.

Gilbert's voice drew quiet and he spoke with an intensity that demanded an audience. "You ask us to stand defenseless in the face of this, my Lord…" the last word carrying a subtle tone of disrespect.

"You ask us to shutter our windows, bar our doors and cower in our beds. What man cowers helplessly in the face of such monstrosity?! What man bows his head and willingly readies himself for death in the throes of such depravity?!" he continued, the crowd gathering tightly behind him.

"We ask you only for our swords, so that we may defend ourselves from this creature, Lord Chambliss. We ask not for more soil from this land, more copper for our chests, or more bread for our fires. We ask you only for the basic right to raise arms against this creature that stalks our people and butchers them like animals… like John Wylde before you…" he finished, eyes cast down at the body before him and then back at

THE BEAST WITHIN

Chambliss.

There was a long pause as Chambliss stared calmly at Gilbert, his cool blue eyes threatening to unnerve the peasant. His lips drew taut and formed a sneer as he began to speak.

"There will be no swords, peasant," he enunciated the last word for effect. "You will disperse this gathering and return to your fields now," he said, nodding almost imperceptibly at his men who in turn lowered their silver pikes to the crowd.

Gilbert cast a final, defiant look at Chambliss and turned just as Nathaniel grasped his sleeve, leading him back towards the hamlet with the sullen crowd.

CHAPTER THREE

I t had been two long years since the beast first took a peasant of Erenwold. On the eve of every full moon since, like the great clocks of Lucius' castle, another friend, sister, or mother departed this world in most gruesome fashion. Gilbert could remember well those early killings, the fear that gripped the town, the unknowing of what vile culprit wrought such carnage, and most of all, when it would be back. Each killing was the same, multiple lacerations across the torso in what looked like the strokes of a giant claw, tearing top to bottom with chunks of flesh gnawed from the neck.

There had been tales of the creature in the

woods surrounding Erenwold since long before the killings began. What exactly it was, no one knew. Only a handful of villagers had claimed sight of the creature. Their descriptions all bore a striking resemblance - wild, covered in matted strands of brown fur, large, wide-set eyes glowing in the night, two heads higher than a man and capable of running on twos or fours. What had turned this creature to rage and bloodlust, no one knew, but before long, the "Beast of Erenwold" had become a thing of legend and the stuff of nightmares.

Gilbert Fogg, for one, was through living the nightmare. From the moment he left the estate of Chambliss with the other peasants, his mind began to set in motion a series of events to end the suffering of Erenwold once and for all; to bring the crimes of the beast to an end whether it cost him his life or not. It was evident that the villagers could rely on no help from their Lord, much less King Lucius, both of whom seemed perfectly content to let the beast have its monthly "meal" at the expense of perhaps a bit more order in the village each day.

It was true that without their swords, the petty squabbles over ale, women, or property that often turned bloody had subsided in large part. *At what cost, though?* wondered Gilbert. Surely a peasant armed with sword or blade would fare better against the Beast of Erenwold, and perhaps it would have been killed by now. It was no use wondering, though. There were no swords to be had and Gilbert knew he would have to make due with the instruments available to him.

Shortly after the gathering before Chambliss, Gilbert had pulled Nathaniel aside to ask his support. The two had spoken little since their retrieval of John Wylde's body. A grim silence hung over the village in general. The full moon would be upon them soon enough, however, and Gilbert knew that he had to act in order to put his plan in motion.

Nathaniel was at first resistant; no two men could face the Beast of Erenwold and survive. They knew little about the creature other than the evidence left on the corpses of its victims.

The two men talked long into the night, a dim candle flickering before them in the back room of Gilbert's shack. Margaret slept quietly in the other room. Eventually, Nathaniel relented, his deep, furrowed brow relaxing somewhat when the decision was finally made. Gilbert had been convincing in his appeals and Nathaniel knew it. It was true, there was no hope of arms, no support from Chambliss and nothing otherwise that would lead to the end of the beast's torment. It was only a matter of time before the beast lay eyes upon his family, perhaps his eldest son, or his wife. Something had to be done and it was better two determined men die trying to save the village than to sit and wait for the dreadful howls in the night to remind them of their cowardice.

CHAPTER FOUR

T he night was uncommonly crisp as a brisk wind blew into Erenwold from the north. On the horizon, just above the span of fields and dilapidated wooden shacks, the full moon began to peak carefully over the woods.

Gilbert and Nathaniel moved with urgency uncommon for simple peasants, pushing swiftly through the undergrowth of the forest, the two of them laboring to carry a heavy, twine net across their shoulders.

"We must hurry, Nathaniel," implored Gilbert, his words spaced by the heaving of his breath. "The moon is rising quickly this eve…"

Nathaniel said nothing, the words not warranting the expenditure of breath. The two men pressed forward through the forest, sweat beading and dripping from their brows.

Eventually, they arrived at a small clearing surrounded by dense foliage at the base of a hill. Gilbert had chosen the spot earlier in the month, having recalled the area where they had found John Wylde's body and having remembered previous screams from these parts of the woods.

Working quickly, they hoisted the large, handspun net high in a nearby tree, its corners weighting the sickly boughs. Gilbert took a length of rope attached to the net and walked backwards fifty paces into the foliage, stopping only to rest his pitchfork at his feet. He turned the rope once around the small trunk of a nearby tree to take the tension off the net and crouched behind some thick bushes. Meanwhile, Nathaniel had retreated to the other side of the clearing, the sharpened end of a gardening tool in his hand. He glanced furtively at Gilbert through the darkness, still wondering how he had drawn lots to coax the creature from the woods.

And so the pair waited, Gilbert holding the end of the line and Nathaniel fifty paces away near the clearing talking loudly to himself, his fears betrayed by the shivering in his voice. He reminded himself that there were no other options. The village and most importantly, his family, depended on them. This deed must be done.

The night passed slowly. The crispness of the air kept both men invigorated. The sky grew blacker as the moon rose high into the night. From the clearing, Nathaniel could see the pale moon inching higher and higher, looking much too placid to be a harbinger of such horrors.

And before long, there it was... the twisting of branches signaling the coming of the beast.

Nathaniel continued to talk, his voice subconsciously dipping to a whisper now as he strained hard to hear every sound as the creature approached. He cast a frightened glance at Gilbert whose eyes had grown wide, a clear expression of intense encouragement on his face.

The noises grew louder now, the crunching of branches and the splitting of vines underfoot of the monster. Nathaniel could barely keep himself from running to the woods in flight.

THE BEAST WITHIN

And then he turned, and it was upon him, just feet from the clearing, not yet within range of the trap.

The creature came stumbling out of the foliage to Nathaniel's right as he instinctively raised his wooden spear, still disbelieving that he had exposed himself to such foolishness.

It rambled out from the bushes on two feet, arms hung low before it and it stopped, staring at Nathaniel as he stared back. If he only lived for but a moment more, Nathaniel had born closest witness to the Beast of Erenwold and he had to admit, it wasn't quite what he had expected.

The creature before him stood tall, much taller than the tallest man in the village, but hunched over it was close to eye level with Nathaniel. Its body was draped with a thick growth of dark fur, brown or black, Nathaniel could not tell. It appeared disheveled and matted, attesting to life in these woods. Its arms hung low and its large fur-covered hands draped just a foot above the ground. It stood and stared, and Nathaniel stared back.

He stared into a wide set of deep, yellow eyes, the pupils large and black. Not the eyes of a maddened beast, it seemed, but rather the eyes of someone, something, lost, something confused. The creature tilted its head slightly, the look a human gives when trying to understand, and it let loose a slow, deep grumble that rose at the end. A dirty set of flattened teeth revealed briefly in the moonlight.

Perhaps not the beast he had expected, but a wolf in sheep's clothing, nonetheless, thought Nathaniel. Raising his wooden spear, he stepped backwards carefully, the creature lumbering very slowly after him, head still cocked and eyes wide.

Just a few more feet, thought Nathaniel. Keep coming...

Gilbert released the rope and with a whoosh, the twine netting came crashing down, pinning the beast below it. The creature let loose a sudden howl when it realized it had been trapped, the sadness of the baying driving deep into Nathaniel's heart. It thrashed and spun, trying to find a way out of the netting.

Gilbert pulled the line taut and tied the netting to the tree with as much energy as he could muster, forearms weak from having held the rope for so long.

THE BEAST WITHIN

"Kill it, Nathaniel!" he cried, turning from the tree to look upon his partner, standing at the edge of the clearing holding his spear.

Rushing from corner to corner, tying the net in place as the creature thrashed, Gilbert shouted once more at Nathaniel.

"Our families, Nathaniel! Kill the beast!" he wailed, his voice unleashing months of brewing anger.

Nathaniel hesitated briefly as he watched the creature flail and claw at the netting, its sad howls echoed in the still night. He thought of John Wylde, his ragged torso, so violently torn, his family left behind.

And then he raised his sharpened stake and began to plunge it at the helpless creature, over and over and over again, working himself into a frenzied bloodlust.

Eventually, the noises stopped and the creature grew still, a lump of fur and netting drenched in the blood of a dozen stab wounds. Nathaniel breathed heavily, the sweat dripping onto his bottom lip. He felt a hand on his shoulder, shaking him from his near hypnotic state.

"We've done it, my friend!" said Gilbert, an

unmistakably joyous ring in the words. "We have ended this nightmare, once and for all!"

Slowly, a smile crept across Nathaniel's face. Not a full smile, but a half smile, of a man who grew more and more comfortable with what he had done. He said nothing and only turned briefly to Gilbert who grasped his shoulders and shook him jubilantly.

"Guard the body, Nathaniel, I am going to the village for Lord Chambliss and his men. They shall see for themselves that you and I have ended this scourge," he said. Nathaniel only nodded, unable to speak as his deep breaths heaved his chest.

Gilbert set forth on the village, his feet moving as swiftly as they could carry him. A pride long-since buried welled deep in his chest.

Margaret would be so proud of him, he thought, and he longed to be with her, to tell her of their night, of their plans and the salvation they had brought to the hamlet. The peacefulness of the village has been preserved and there was sure to be accolades and tokens of thankfulness from the other peasants. His thoughts carried him onwards to Erenwold, ignoring the burning in his lungs and the aching in his body.

THE BEAST WITHIN

He pressed forward through the foliage una-bated by such things.

And then the night was shattered.

The unmistakable shrieking of a human voice behind him - Nathaniel's voice - howled in almost inhuman agony.

Gilbert stopped abruptly, his leg twisting awkwardly over the root of a birch tree. *The beast had not been dead after all! How could he have left Nathaniel alone with the creature?!* He had been sure it was dead, a dozen wounds sprouting the sanguine testament to its demise.

None of it mattered now as he turned back towards the clearing, legs and arms pumping furiously to propel him forward through the forest.

The screams had ceased by the time Gilbert neared the clearing, his lungs gasping for oxy-gen. He clutched his pitchfork tightly with both hands. If there was any hope to save Nathaniel, he was it. He had coaxed Nathaniel to join him, the more timid man giving way to his pleadings. It was Gilbert's time to face the beast and face him he would.

Pressing forward through the last remnants

of the forest, Gilbert could hear muffled noises, the dense foliage largely absorbing the sounds in the clearing. Whether Nathaniel lived or not, the creature would face the sharpened points of Gilbert's pitchfork once and for all.

Brushing aside the last tangles of the forest, Gilbert stepped defiantly into the clearing to face the Beast of Erenwold and stopped suddenly in his tracks.

The cold, wispy breaths of a half dozen dark horses filled the clearing before him as Gilbert's eyes grew wide in disbelief. Perched high on the imposing steeds and turning to face him stood a handful of heavily armored soldiers, their figures completely cloaked in darkened armor, bearing a familiar crest.

The crest of King Lucius of Devon.

His eyes quickly cast down from the riders before him, looking quickly for the beast, and for his friend, Nathaniel. There, slumped lifeless beside the tangled corpse of the beast, lay Nathaniel, his torso torn diagonally from shoulder to hip with the familiar curved lacerations of the beast. And kneeled beside Nathaniel was a darkened figure, head tilted downwards, long, dark hair veiling his face.

THE BEAST WITHIN

Gilbert stared in the horror and confusion of a man whose mind could simply not process the scene before him, as the figure lifted its head, the wild, black hair falling to either side of his face.

King Lucius looked upon Gilbert with the eyes of a ravening madman. His gaze was devoid of humanity and his mouth was soiled with the blood of Nathaniel Bedford.

With his last ounce of consciousness, Gilbert turned slightly back to the riders, at the sound of metal being unsheathed. Their wicked curved blades fell upon him as the moon hung solemnly over Erenwold.

BEHIND THE
WALLS
OF MADNESS

BEHIND THE WALLS OF MADNESS

H is eyes shot open wide at the interminable scratching. The room was black and dead, not yet adorned by the morning light.

The noise grew louder now — insufferable. Its thick, rotted fingernails dragged frantically across the inside of the thin drywall, signaling an end to their macabre truce. He pulled the covers back and sat up in bed, exhausted.

For three straight days, the scratching had grown louder and more frequent, clawing and itching restlessly from inside the wall. Now, it was in his bedroom, just past the foot of his bed. He could hear its wretched fingers running up and down the wall, as if looking for a seam to escape from the bowels of this cursed house.

"Stop it!!!" he shrieked madly into the darkness at the thing.

The noises stopped and the room grew still once more. In the blackness, there was only the sound of the old, metal fan as it whirred its monotonous cadence, unperturbed by the thing in the wall.

He pressed his hands hard to the side of his head, struggling to suppress the fury that welled within him. The clock read 4:17AM. Eyes strained wide with stress, he turned over his left shoulder and glanced at the window. Behind the cracked and bent vertical blinds, the night lingered tentatively outside, awaiting the impatient dawn.

He lay back down in the bed and rested his head on the rumpled pillow, pulling the thick covers over him. Closing his eyes, he tried to will himself to sleep, but his mind raced in residual fury at the thing behind the wall. For an hour, he curled in bed motionless, eyes determinedly closed against the expectant disruption. Finally, as the soft chirping of the dawn birds filled his ears, he fell asleep once more.

Krrrrrrrrrrrrrrrr…

He was screaming in a rage before his eyes even opened, his mind never fully convinced at the genuineness of his sleep.

BEHIND THE WALLS OF MADNESS

"No!!!" he shrieked, uncontrollably. "Leave me alone!!!"

The thin, metal bedframe rattled beneath him at the sudden outburst. He cocked his right arm quickly and slammed it thunderously backward, pounding on the wall behind him. The drywall cracked and buckled in the shape of his balled fist.

A few seconds of silence taunted him and then the scratching resumed several feet to his right, as if his rage had merely pushed the thing further down the wall. It was clawing incessantly now, maddeningly invisible behind just an inch of drywall.

He flung his legs over the side of the bed and rose quickly to his feet. In the faltering darkness, he kicked around for his slippers and found them. *I will end this once and for all*, he thought.

Marching across the long bedroom and down the hall, he headed straight for the kitchen. The long, halogen bulb flickered hesitantly above, shattering the darkness with its unforgiving light. He clawed at the kitchen drawer like some raving madman, yanking it open. Inside, a collection of silverware slid violently on bare wood and clunked against the end of the draw in a heap. His eyes fell upon the first sharpened blade he saw and he reached in, grabbing a small paring knife.

In the grueling months of this ordeal, he had seen the horrible thing just once. Its monstrous face, set above a pale and sickly frame, had leered at him through the round hole in the bathroom wall.

The muscles on his forearm rippled as he clutched the knife tightly and stormed from the kitchen, heading back down the hall. Reaching around the corner of the bathroom with his right arm, he flipped upward wildly with his fingers. The lights illuminated the small space, covered unfashionably in dated peach and teal tile.

In the close confines of the tiny bathroom, his mind grew clear and still. He stared downward at the old, beige rug and focused, slowing his breathing to concentrate. He could hear the scratching again, coming from just behind the chipped, circular mirror on the wall.

Turning toward the smeared and dusty glass, he raised the knife and inhaled deeply. The serenity of this final act settled over him in a pure, calming wave. He plunged the paring knife deep into the thing, his balled fist slamming into pasty flesh, driving the short blade deep into its core. Again and again, he raised his arm, thrusting the blade into the thing with the unabated rage of many long, sleepless nights. Blood sprayed in crimson arcs across the bathroom, splattering the mirror and staining the peach tile with bright blotches of red. Finally, he stopped and stood there gasping at the exertion. He listened. Beyond the rapid heaving of his breath and the pooling of blood on the cold tile, he heard nothing.

Then, his balled fist weakened and the knife fell from his hands, clattering on the bathroom floor. His heavy eyes looked up toward the mirror. There in the reflection, he saw himself. His pale, bare chest was splattered with blood, stretched outwards like red ribbons from a half-dozen gaping wounds drawn about his torso. His bright, red blood rushed forth and soaked into the beige carpet.

He wobbled and his knees buckled. Like some sad puppet whose final show had ended in a chorus of disdain, he slumped backward against the wall in a miserable, crumpled heap. The final remnants of his life poured from him and ran like a river down the cracks between the tiles.

From just beyond the wall, the thing watched him through a rusted vent, its small, beady eyes thoughtfully observing his last, labored breaths. It cocked its head quizzically and twitched its whiskers, curiously absorbing the unexpected madness. And then, it turned and ran back into the wall, its long, fleshy tail disappearing into the blackness of the house.

THANK YOU

If you found these stories entertaining, please consider leaving a review wherever you purchased this book. More reviews will help more readers find and enjoy these stories.

If you would like to explore my other books and receive a free short story based on the events of "Chasing the Blue Sky", please visit:

www.lomackpublishing.com.

Thank you again for giving up your valuable time to read these stories. I hope you found the time well-spent.

WILL LOWREY

ABOUT THE AUTHOR

Will Lowrey is an attorney and animal rights advocate from Richmond, Virginia. He holds a Juris Doctor from Vermont Law School and a Bachelor of Science from Virginia Commonwealth University. For close to two decades, both before and after law school, Will has been actively involved in animal causes. His experiences include deployments to assist animals in disasters, the closure of roadside zoos, caring for animals from dog and cock fighting cases, community outreach for low income pet owners in areas ranging from urban neighborhoods to Native American reservations, animal rights protests, animal sheltering, public records campaigns against large institutions conducting animal research, and countless other adventures.

In 2018, Will founded Lomack Publishing to promote the rights, interests, and dignity of animals through self-published literature. Will is also the author of *"Chasing the Blue Sky" and "Words on a Killing"* through Lomack Publishing as well as *"We the Pit Bull: The Fate of Pit Bulls*

Under the United States Constitution" published in the Lewis and Clark Animal Law Review Journal, Volume 24, Issue 2.

While most of Will's writing focuses on animal causes, he has dabbled in other areas, writing *"Simple Strategies for the Bar Exam,"* a guide for law students and attorneys taking the bar exam as well as "The Tenebrous Mind," a collection of horror stories.

Will enjoys hearing from readers. If you'd like to contact him, please visit:

www.lomackpublishing.com